Bronwyn Butterfly

Buffy Bumblebee

Caleb Caterpillar

Cassidy Cockroach

Cecilia Centipede

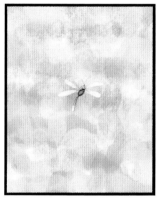

Gnick Gnat

Hakeem Hercules Beetle

Herman Housefly

Jessica Jumping Spider

Liberty Ladybug

Sandy Snail

Savannah Scorpion

Seth Silverfish

Tyson Termite

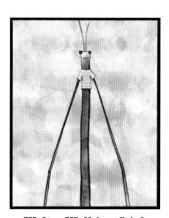

Walter Walking Stick

For all the weird, wonderful critters
(including you)

Published by Roaring Brook Press
Roaring Brook Press is a division of Holtzbrinck Publishing Holdings Limited Partnership
120 Broadway, New York, NY 10271 • mackids.com

Library of Congress Cataloging-in-Publication Data
Names: Pett, Mark, author, illustrator. I Title: I eat poop / Mark Pett.
Description: First edition. I New York : Roaring Brook Press, 2021. I Audience: Ages 3–6. I Audience: Grades K–1.
Summary: A poop-loving dung beetle learns not to hide the quirks that make him special.
Identifiers: LCCN 2020039911 I ISBN 9781250785633 (hardcover)
Subjects: CYAC: Dung beetles—Fiction. I Insects—Fiction. I Individual differences—Fiction. I Popularity—Fiction. I Schools—Fiction.
Classification: LCC PZ7.P4478 Iah 2021 I DDC [E]—dc23
LC record available at https://lccn.loc.gov/2020039911

Our books may be purchased in bulk for promotional, educational, or business use.
Please contact your local bookseller or the Macmillan Corporate and Premium Sales Department
at (800) 221-7945 ext. 5442 or by email at MacmillanSpecialMarkets@macmillan.com.

First edition, 2021 • Book design by Jen Keenan
The illustrations for this book were created digitally.

Printed in China by Hung Hing Off-set Printing Co. Ltd., Heshan City, Guangdong Province

1 3 5 7 9 10 8 6 4 2

I Eat Poop.

A Dung Beetle Story

Mark Pett

Roaring Brook Press
New York

Tuesday began like most days.

I sat down for breakfast with my parents.

As usual, my baby brother was making a mess.

I helped my mom make my favorite lunch—a poop sandwich with the crusts cut off—and I packed up my backpack for school.

At school, as I do every day, I hid my lunch under the big pebble behind the monkey bars, where no one would see it.

It's hard being the only dung beetle in the entire school.

I can't eat lunch with the other kids. I have to sneak snacks at recess. And I have to tell everyone I'm just a regular old ground beetle.

It's a lot of work keeping my secret, but I just don't have a choice. Look how they treat Sammy Stink Bug!

If everyone found out I eat poop, I'd be an outcast!

Dad says I come from a long line of proud dung beetles. He says we help process waste and make the earth more inhabitable.

All I know is, I go through more mouthwash than any kid should.

Dudley Dung Beetle poses with his record-setting ball of dung.

Great-Aunt Dorothy navigates using the Milky Way.

Don't get me wrong—I love poop. As Dad says, it's in my genes. But I wish I were a wasp. Or better yet, a dragonfly.

They are by far the most popular bugs in school.

That's why what happened in Mr. Longlegs's class was so crazy.

One of the popular bugs dropped a stack of books to surprise Ronald Roly Poly.

Ronald snapped into a ball.

He rolled down the aisle, right toward me!

Without thinking, I jumped on top.

I started steering him with my legs . . .

and carefully brought him to a stop.

As I hopped down, the whole class cheered!

"You should sit with us at lunch," said Wesley Wasp.

I couldn't believe it!

For the first time in my life,
I was going to sit with the popular bugs!

When I got to the lunchroom, I didn't even care that I couldn't eat in front of the other bugs.

I walked past Herman Housefly.

As usual, he was sitting alone.

Herman is the only one in school
who knows my secret.

We used to play together,
and we loved the same snacks.

For a while, we were best friends.

As I passed him, Herman said, "Hey, Dougie, want to join me? I've got a poopsicle with your name on it."

"Herman, how can you eat that in front of the other bugs?" I asked. "They'll torture you for it!"

Herman chuckled. "If I let those pests run my life, I'd be miserable."

I joined the popular bugs at their table and pretended I wasn't hungry.

By afternoon recess, my abdomen was really growling!

I snuck away to find my lunch sack under the big pebble behind the monkey bars.

As I opened the sack, I heard a voice.

"What's that?" It was Gnick Gnat, the peskiest bug in school.

"Er, I don't know," I lied. "I just found it under this pebble."

The popular bugs gathered around.

"Open it," said Derek Dragonfly.

"Yeah, let's see what's in it," said Wesley Wasp.

My antennae went numb as I pulled out my lunch, item by item.

"Ew, gross!" said Gnick. "It's a poop sandwich!"

"And poop pudding!" said Derek.

"And a box of poop juice!" added Wesley.

"This is disgusting," said Gnick.
"Who do you think it belongs to?"

"Probably that housefly," said Wesley.
"He's the only one in school
who eats poop."

"There he is!" said Derek.

"You should go dump it on his head," said Wesley.

Bugs from across the playground
started swarming around us.

As they urged me on, I crept up behind Herman.

I felt a pounding in my thorax.

I was about to humiliate my old friend.

I stopped and turned around.

"I can't," I said. "It's *my* lunch."

The crowd gasped.

"Yours?" said Wesley. "You like poop?"

"I do," I admitted. "I love it. It's the first thing I want to eat in the morning, and the last thing I want to eat at night. It's my favorite thing in the whole wide world."

Then I did something I never thought I'd do.

I took a bite of my sandwich. In front of everyone.

"Look at him!" shrieked Gnick. "He loves it!"

"That's so gross!" said Derek.

But I was shocked by what happened next.

A second-grader praying mantis spoke up.

"So? My mom ate my dad."

Everyone looked at each other.

"I have ears in my armpits," said Manuel Moth.

"I eat dead people," said Maude Maggot.

"I throw up when people touch me," said Gareth Grasshopper.

"I was born pregnant," said Alphonse Aphid.

"I breathe through my butt," said Tammy Tick.

It turned out, the whole school was crawling with weirdos!

Even the popular bugs turned out to be weird.

The next morning I went to school carrying my Captain Dung Beetle lunch box.

And I've eaten in the lunchroom with my friends ever since.

Adam Ant
Choir
Can carry many times his weight

Aisha Acorn Weevil
Drill Team
Uses snout to drill into acorns

Alphonse Aphid
Mathlete
Poops sugar

Bob Bombardier Beetle
Debate Team
Squirts boiling-hot liquid
from butt

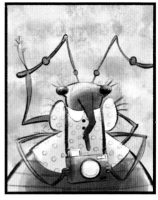

Britney Bedbug
Photography Club
Can go for a year without eating

Courtney Camel Spider
Rugby Team
Jaw makes up 30% of her body

Dougie Dung Beetle
Soccer Team
Can push 1000 times
his own weight

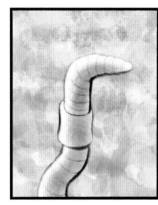

Earl Earthworm
Gardening Club
Has five hearts

Felicia Firefly
Drama Club
Lights up butt to say hello

Gareth Grasshopper
Track & Field
Has ears on his belly

Manuel Moth
Drama Club
Can smell another
moth miles away

Molly Mosquito
Health Club
Beats wings 300–600 times
per second

Penelope Praying Mantis
Softball Team
Only insect capable of
swiveling her head

Ronald Roly Poly
Soccer Team
Drinks water through both
ends of his body

Sammy Stink Bug
Golf Team
Farts when frightened